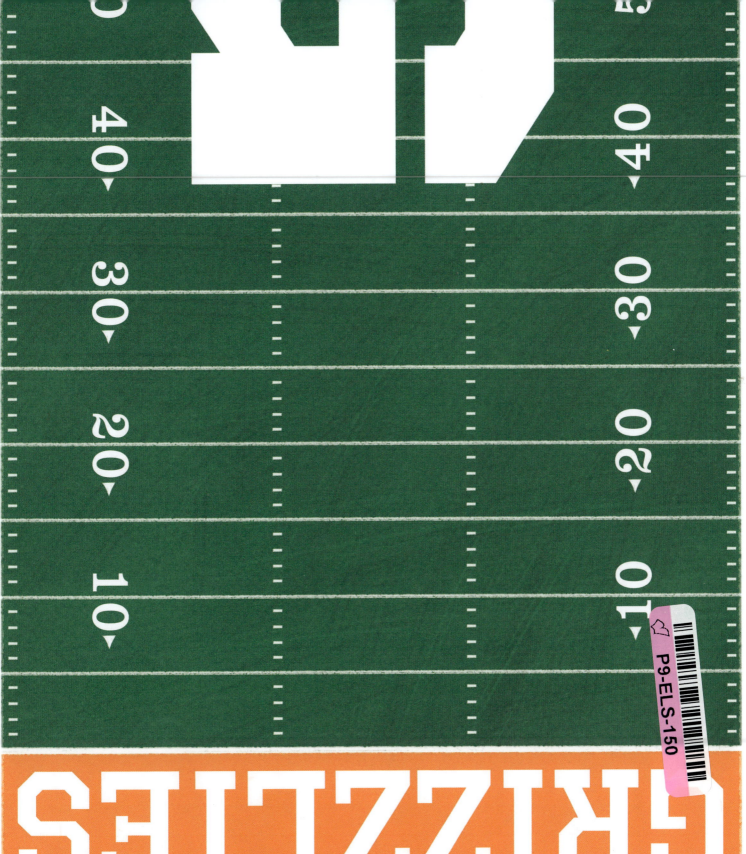

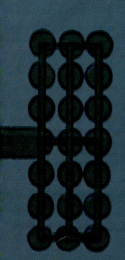

GOODNIGHT
FOOTBALL

BY MICHAEL DAHL

ILLUSTRATED BY CHRISTINA FORSHAY

CAPSTONE
YOUNG READERS

Sports
Illustrated
KIDS

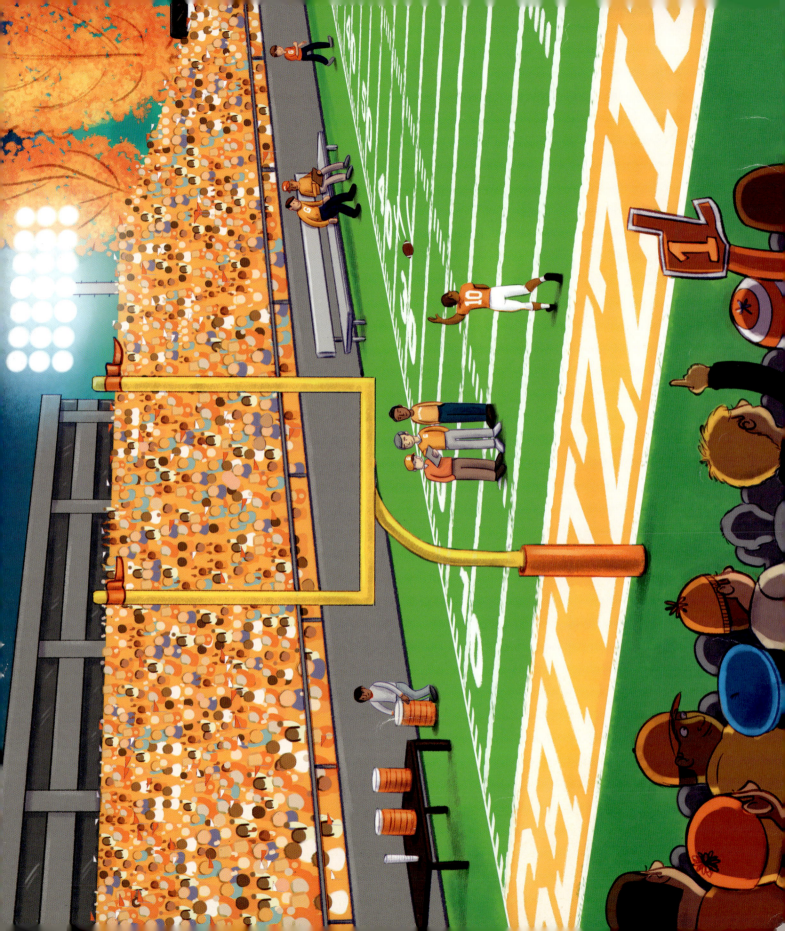

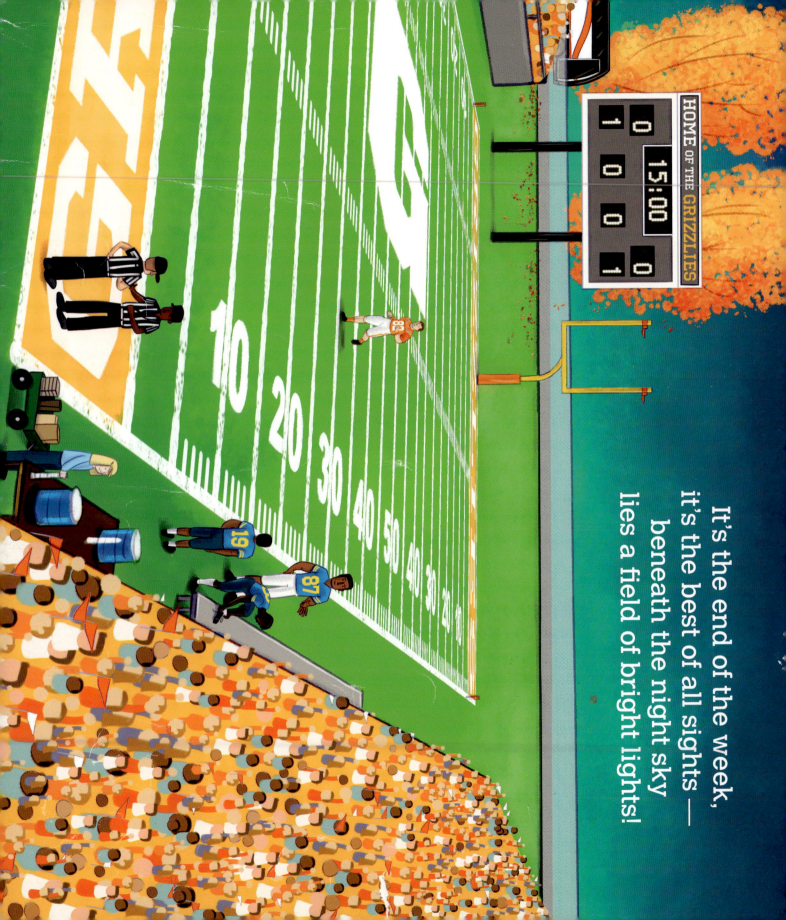

It's the end of the week,
it's the best of all sights —
beneath the night sky
lies a field of bright lights!

And the bleachers are full, for a very good reason.

The big game is tonight! It's football season!

The big band plays, and the cheerleaders shout!

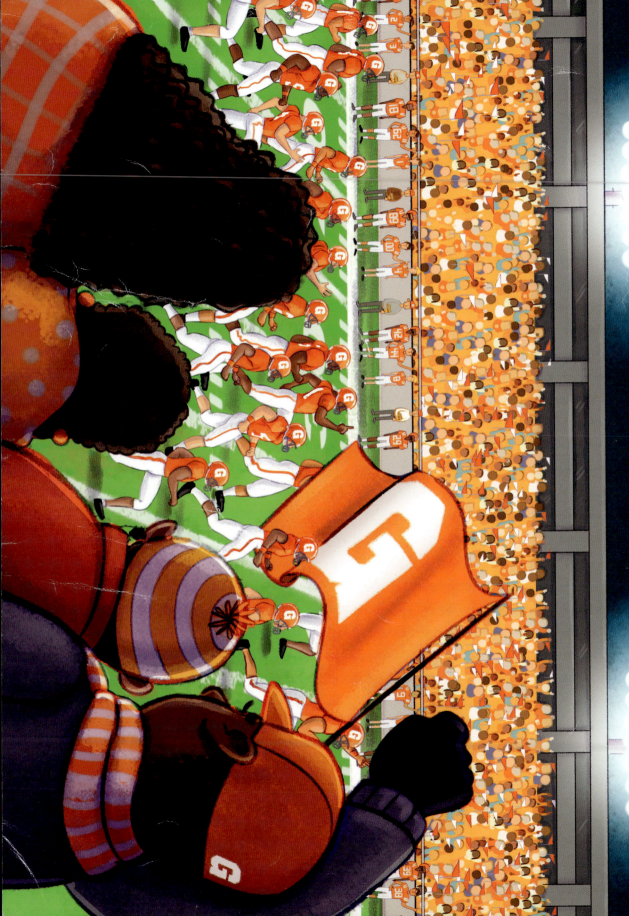

And everyone
cheers as the
teams run out!

The fans are excited.
It's time for some fun!

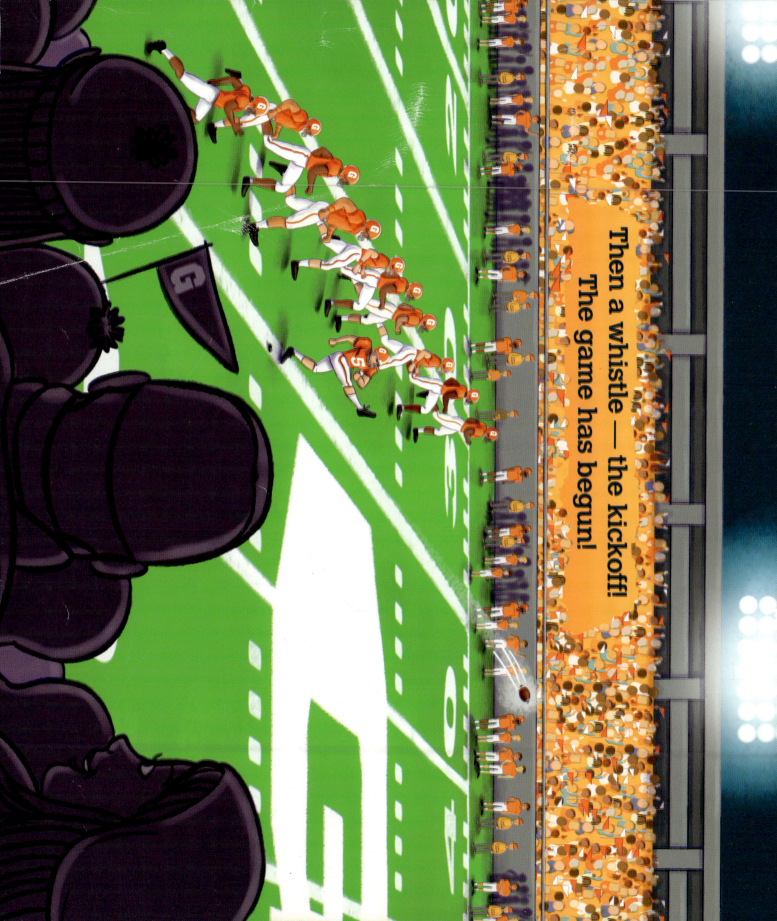

Then a whistle — the kickoff!
The game has begun!

On third and one, the ball is snapped.

Then the team huddles up and discusses a play.

The quarterback drops back and lets the ball go.

It sails through the air.

Oh, what a throw!

A receiver
breaks loose
and stands all
alone . . .

reaches up . . .
grabs the ball . . .

he's in the end zone!

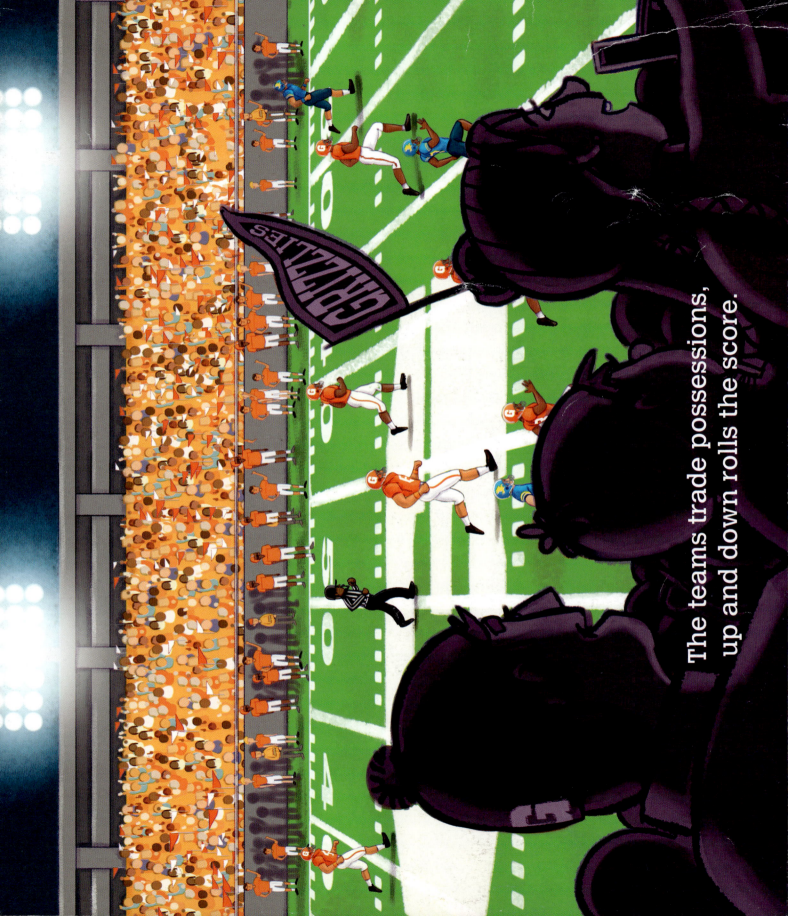

The teams trade possessions,
up and down rolls the score.

Then a long run wins the game —
hear the crowd ROAR!

What a game! What a night!

Goodnight, players. You fought a good fight.

Goodnight coaches, as they shake hands.

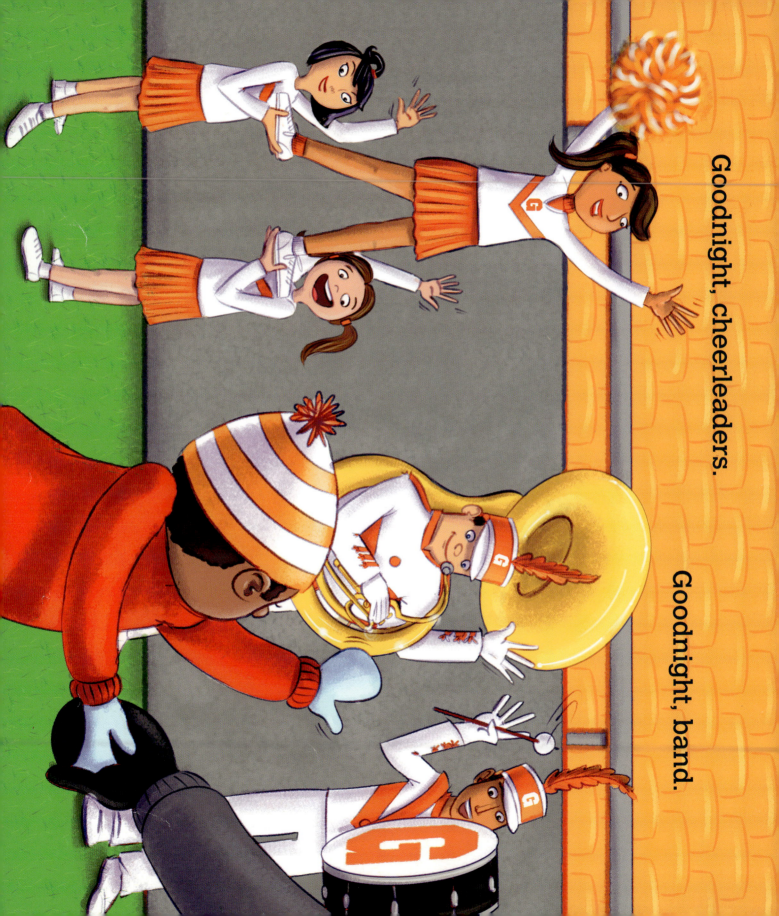

Goodnight, cheerleaders.

Goodnight, band.

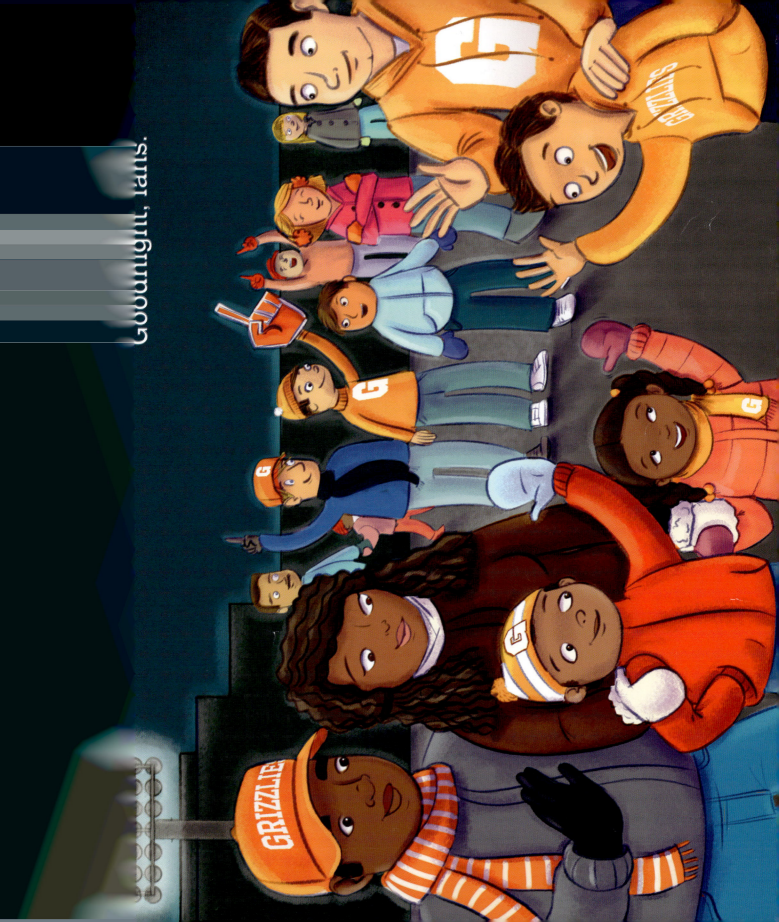

Goodnight, fans.

Go during field and plein intfigld and concession stands.

Goodnight, mascot.

We'll come back soon.

Goodnight, goalposts.
Goodnight, moon.

Goodnight helmet
and my favorite
teams . . .

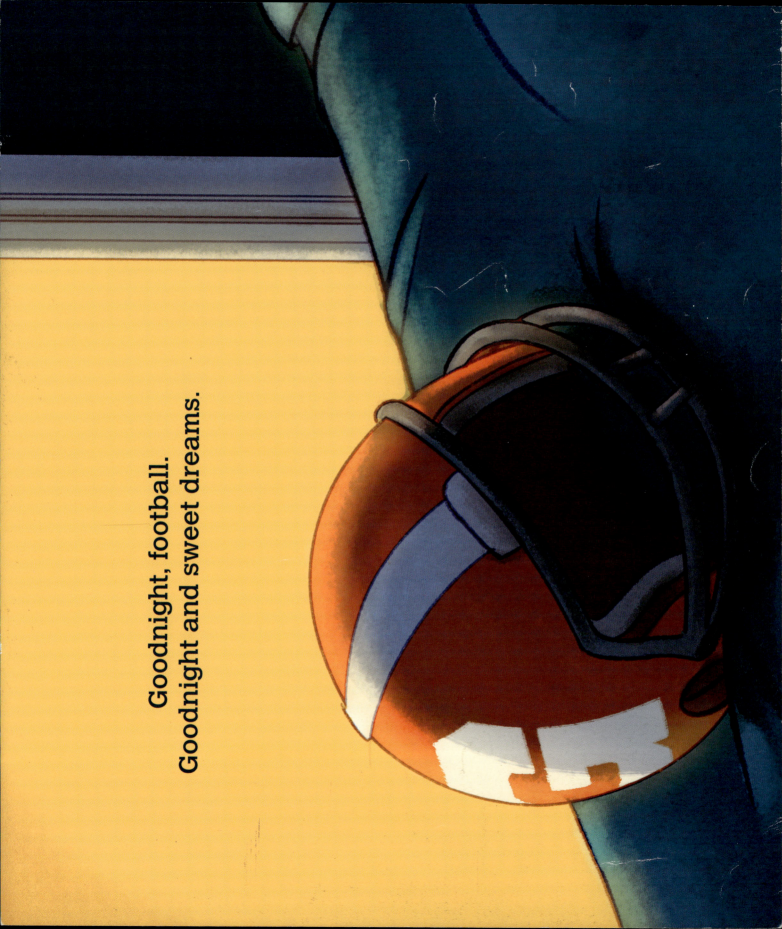

Goodnight, football.
Goodnight and sweet dreams.

TO DANNY THOMAS.

Published by
CAPSTONE YOUNG READERS
a Capstone imprint
1710 Roe Crest Drive, North Mankato, Minnesota 56003
www.capstoneyoungreaders.com

Library of Congress Cataloging-in-Publication data is available on the Library of Congress website.

ISBN: 978-1-62370-106-2 (hardcover)
ISBN: 978-1-4795-5177-4 (library binding)
ISBN: 978-1-4795-5186-6 (paperback)
ISBN: 978-1-4795-55962-6 (ebook)

Designer: Bob Lentz

Printed in the United States of America in
North Mankato, Minnesota.
072016   009898R

40 40

30 30

20 20

10 10

GRIZZLIES